Published by Magna Books
Magna Road
Wigston
Leicester LE18 4ZH

Produced by
Twin Books UK Ltd
Kimbolton House
117A Fulham Road
London SW3 6RL

© 1992 Twin Books UK

Directed by CND – Muriel Nathan-Deiller
Illustrated by VAn Gool-Lefévre-Loiseaux

ISBN 1 85422 430 1

Printed in Hong Kong

"'VAN GOOL'S'"

Pinocchio

MAGNA BOOKS

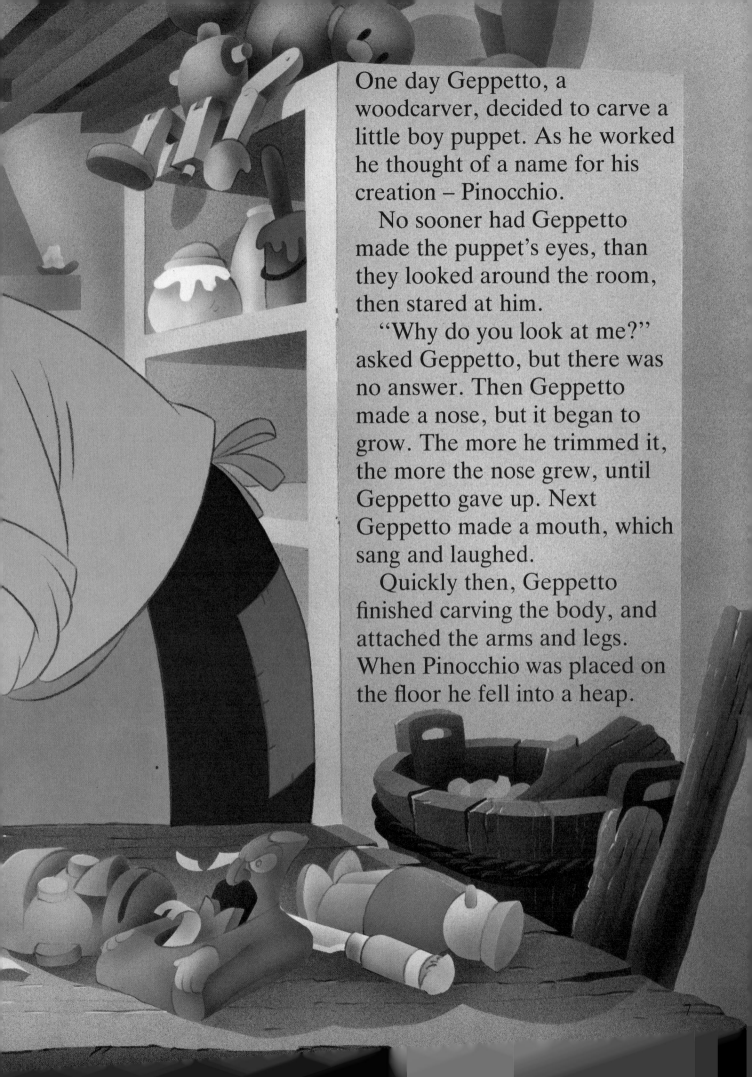

One day Geppetto, a woodcarver, decided to carve a little boy puppet. As he worked he thought of a name for his creation – Pinocchio.

No sooner had Geppetto made the puppet's eyes, than they looked around the room, then stared at him.

"Why do you look at me?" asked Geppetto, but there was no answer. Then Geppetto made a nose, but it began to grow. The more he trimmed it, the more the nose grew, until Geppetto gave up. Next Geppetto made a mouth, which sang and laughed.

Quickly then, Geppetto finished carving the body, and attached the arms and legs. When Pinocchio was placed on the floor he fell into a heap.

7

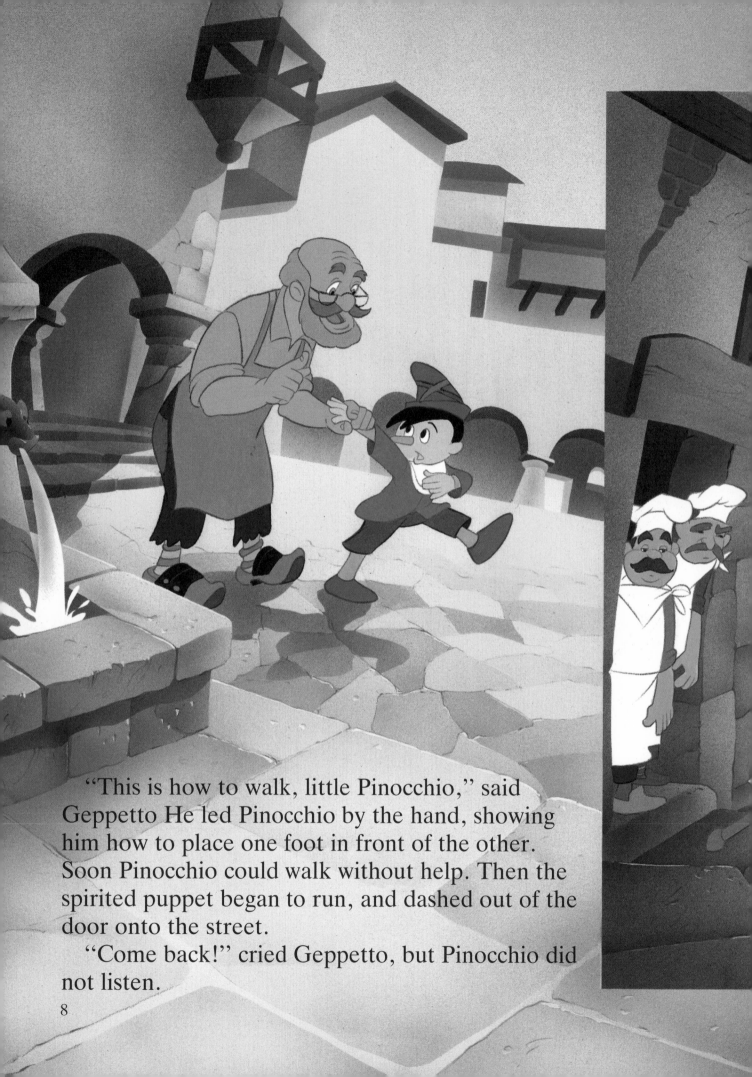

"This is how to walk, little Pinocchio," said Geppetto He led Pinocchio by the hand, showing him how to place one foot in front of the other. Soon Pinocchio could walk without help. Then the spirited puppet began to run, and dashed out of the door onto the street.

"Come back!" cried Geppetto, but Pinocchio did not listen.

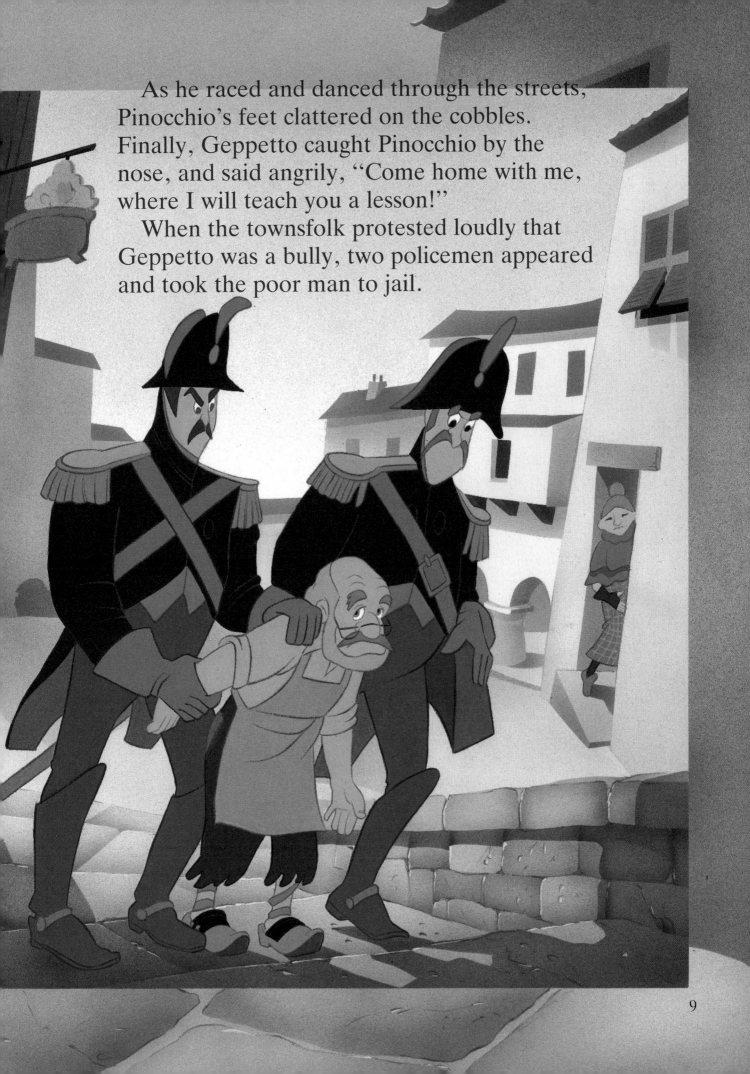

As he raced and danced through the streets, Pinocchio's feet clattered on the cobbles. Finally, Geppetto caught Pinocchio by the nose, and said angrily, "Come home with me, where I will teach you a lesson!"

When the townsfolk protested loudly that Geppetto was a bully, two policemen appeared and took the poor man to jail.

Pinocchio didn't feel at all sorry that he had caused Geppetto such trouble. The little puppet returned home. Suddenly, he heard a voice. "*Cri-cri-cri*. Learn to be good."

"Who said that?" asked Pinocchio, frightened.

"It's me, the cricket," answered the voice.

Pinocchio saw an enormous cricket sitting on the mantlepiece. "A cricket! What are you doing here?"

"I live here," said the cricket. "And I have to tell you, that you should learn to listen and to be kind to others."

"Oh, be quiet!" shouted Pinocchio rudely and he turned away.

By now it was dark outside, and Pinocchio was hungry.
He searched the room but could not find a scrap of food.
About to give up, Pinocchio finally found an egg. But when
the eager puppet tried to crack the egg into a pan, a chick
opped out, ran off the table, and flew out the window.

The hungry puppet went into the village and banged on
a door. A grumpy man in a nightshirt came to the window.
"What do you want? It's late!" he shouted.

"Please, would you give me a piece of bread?" asked Pinocchio.

"Wait here," replied the man. He thought Pinocchio was one of
those mischievous boys who rings people's doorbells at night just
to bother them. He returned to the window and dumped a bucket
of water on the poor puppet, drenching him from head to toe. 13

Now Pinocchio was wet, as well as tired and hungry. He ran home and sat on a stool. To warm his feet he put them on the brazier – a pan filled with burning coals – and fell asleep at once. But while he slept, his little wooden feet caught fire, and smouldered to ashes.

In the morning Pinocchio was awakened by a loud banging at the door.

"It's Geppetto! Open up!" shouted an angry voice.

But when Pinocchio jumped up to unlock the door, he fell flat. Geppetto had to climb in through the window.

Geppetto was furious at having been thrown in jail on Pinocchio's account, but when he saw his little puppet lying helplessly with no feet, his heart softened. He carved a fine pair of little feet and attached them to Pinocchio's legs.

"Now don't run away on these new feet!"
cautioned Geppetto.

"I won't, papa," replied Pinocchio. "I'll try to do
things right, now. I'll even go to school."

"That's a good boy," said Geppetto proudly.

Then Pinocchio tucked a book under his arm and
started out for school.

Pinocchio talked to himself as he walked. "This time," he said, "I'll do just as papa says. I'll go to school and learn to read and write."

But Pinocchio began to hear music, and he stopped to listen. Then, forgetting about school, he followed the sound until he came to a puppet show, surrounded by a crowd of people.

The show was so funny and lively that soon Pinocchio was laughing with everyone else. His delight and excitement grew until, carried away, he leaped on to the stage. The stringless puppet drew such a thunderous applause for his antics that when the show ended the puppeteer gave Pinocchio five gold pieces. "Give them to your poor father," he said.

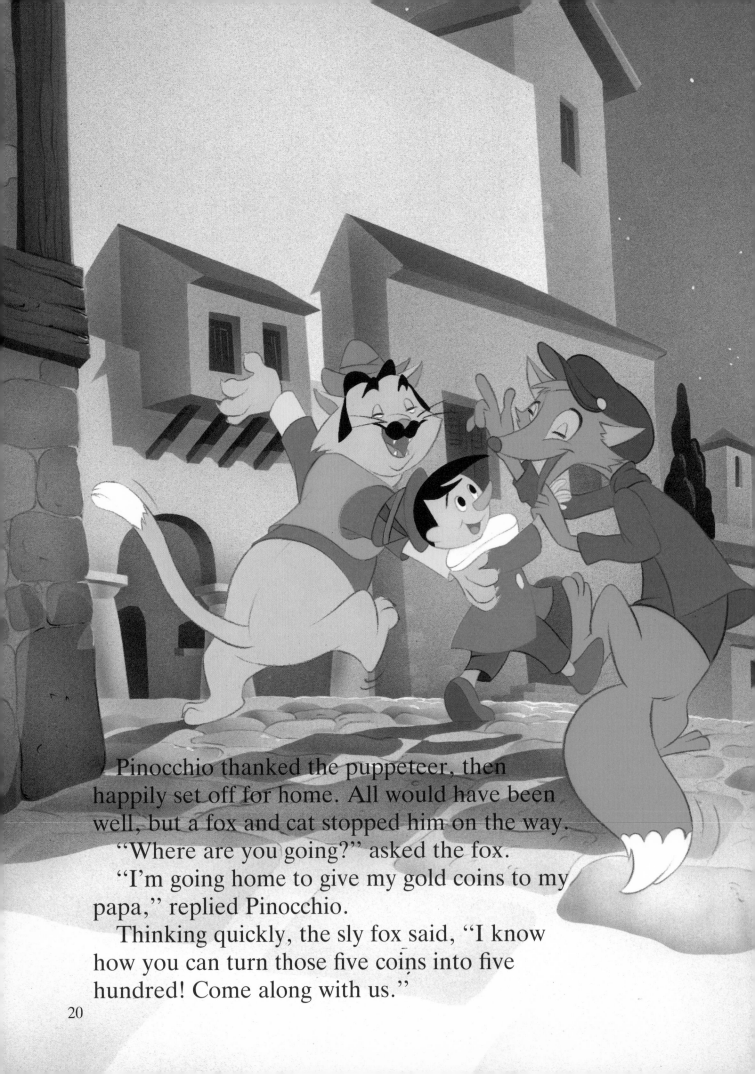

Pinocchio thanked the puppeteer, then happily set off for home. All would have been well, but a fox and cat stopped him on the way.

"Where are you going?" asked the fox.

"I'm going home to give my gold coins to my papa," replied Pinocchio.

Thinking quickly, the sly fox said, "I know how you can turn those five coins into five hundred! Come along with us."

At first, Pinocchio objected, saying his papa was waiting for him, and he had already been naughty enough to skip school. But the thought of five hundred gold coins danced in his head, and he soon agreed to join the fox and cat. They brought him to an inn, where they feasted royally, using one of Pinocchio's coins, and explained the plan.

"You plant your coins in the Field of Miracles," said the fox. "And in the morning you'll find a tree, loaded with more coins than you can count!"

Their plan was to sleep at the inn until midnight, then go plant the coins. The tired little Pinocchio fell deep asleep, and dreamed of trees full of gold coins, tinkling in the breeze. But when Pinocchio awoke, his friends were gone.

"I will find the Field of Miracles myself," thought the puppet. "Maybe my friends are waiting for me there."

Taking the four gold coins he had left, Pinocchio set off down the path. He was surprised to meet the talking cricket along the way.

"What are you doing here?" asked Pinocchio

"I'm here to give you some advice," replied the cricket. "Go home now to poor Geppetto, and give him your coins. He's terribly sad because he misses you and wonders where you are."

"But tomorrow my papa will be rich!" said the puppet.

Pinocchio would not listen to the cricket, and continued on his way. He was busy thinking of things he would buy with his money, when he heard footsteps behind him. Pinocchio turned to look, and saw two figures, about the same size as the fox and cat, wearing masks and following him. As he began to run, they chased after him.

Pinocchio ran for miles, the hoodlums close behind. He was ready to drop with exhaustion when he saw a house far in the distance. He headed for the house fast as he could run, and soon he could see a woman standing at the window. She had blue hair.

"Let me in!" cried Pinocchio. "They're after me!"

25

But just then the hoodlums grabbed his shoulders and spun him around. "Your money or your life," said one of them gruffly. But Pinocchio couldn't speak because he had the coins under his tongue.

"Alright then," said the other, "we'll fix him!"

They hanged poor Pinocchio in a tree, but when he didn't die right away they grew tired of waiting. "We'll come back tomorrow, fool," said one of them as they left.

Pinocchio hanged for a long time. He hope someone would save him. He thought of his papa, and wished he had listened to the cricket. Then the puppet closed his eyes. He didn't see the animal servants of the blue-haired woman coming to take him from the tree. They brought Pinocchio to her house, where the woman gently placed him on a bed.

"Is he alive?" asked the owl.

"I don't know," replied the blue-haired woman, who was really a kind fairy. Just then Pinocchio began to shiver and shake.

"I know that puppet," said the cricket. "He is a naughty rascal who won't listen, and will make his poor papa die of a broken heart."

When the animals left the room, the Blue Fairy asked, "Why aren't you home with your papa, like a good boy?"

"It's not my fault," said Pinocchio. "The cat and fox made me go with them." As soon as Pinocchio said this, his nose began to grow.

"You lie is as plain as the nose on your face," laughed the Fairy.

"Please fix my nose!" cried the puppet. "I promise not to lie again."

Pinocchio's nose returned to its normal size.
He thanked the Fairy for her help, and set off to
go straight home to his papa. But he approached
the hanging tree, he saw the fox and cat.

"Ah, Pinocchio! Are you ready now to go to
the Field of Miracles?" called the fox.

"Why did you disappear from the inn last night? When I tried to find the field, two robbers tried to kill me," said Pinocchio.

"We had to see a sick relative," lied the cat.

"But we're together again!" exclaimed the fox. And they convinced the puppet to go with them to the Field of Miracles, where he planted his coins.

"We must be going, now," said the fox.

"Good luck to you," said the cat.

"Good-bye, and thank you!" called Pinocchio as they left. Then he lay down happily on the ground, and fell fast asleep, dreaming again of riches.

When Pinocchio awoke the next morning, he could not see a tree of gold coins anywhere. "Where are all my coins?" he wondered aloud.

"Gone! Long gone!" answered a parrot, perched in the tree nearby. "The cat and fox dug them up while you slept, and ran away."

Pinocchio's mouth dropped open, and then he stamped his feet and cried.

Sad and ashamed, Pinocchio decided to return to the Blue Fairy, who had been so kind to him. He ran back along the path, but when at last he came to where the house had stood, there was only a gravestone in its place.

Pinocchio fell to his knees and sobbed.

"Come back, Blue Fairy!" he lamented.

Just then an enormous pigeon landed nearby. "Have you seen a puppet named Pinocchio in your travels?" asked the bird.

"I'm Pinocchio!" answered the puppet.

"Come with me, then," said the pigeon. "Geppetto is setting out to sea to look for you."

Pinocchio dried his tears, climbed on to the pigeon's back, and away they flew.

The pigeon and Pinocchio travelled all day, and then all night, before reaching the coast. Pinocchio slid off the pigeon's back, but when he turned to thank him, the kind bird had already flown away. The little puppet looked across the wide stretch of blue ocean, and caught sight of a little boat with a man in it, bobbing in the waves.

"Papa!" screamed Pinocchio. But just then a bog wave swamped the boat, which disappeared. "I'll save you!" shouted the puppet, diving into the sea. Pinocchio swam for a long time, and just when he thought his strength would give out, he reached an island. A dolphin near the shore told the puppet that Geppetto had been swallowed by a huge shark.

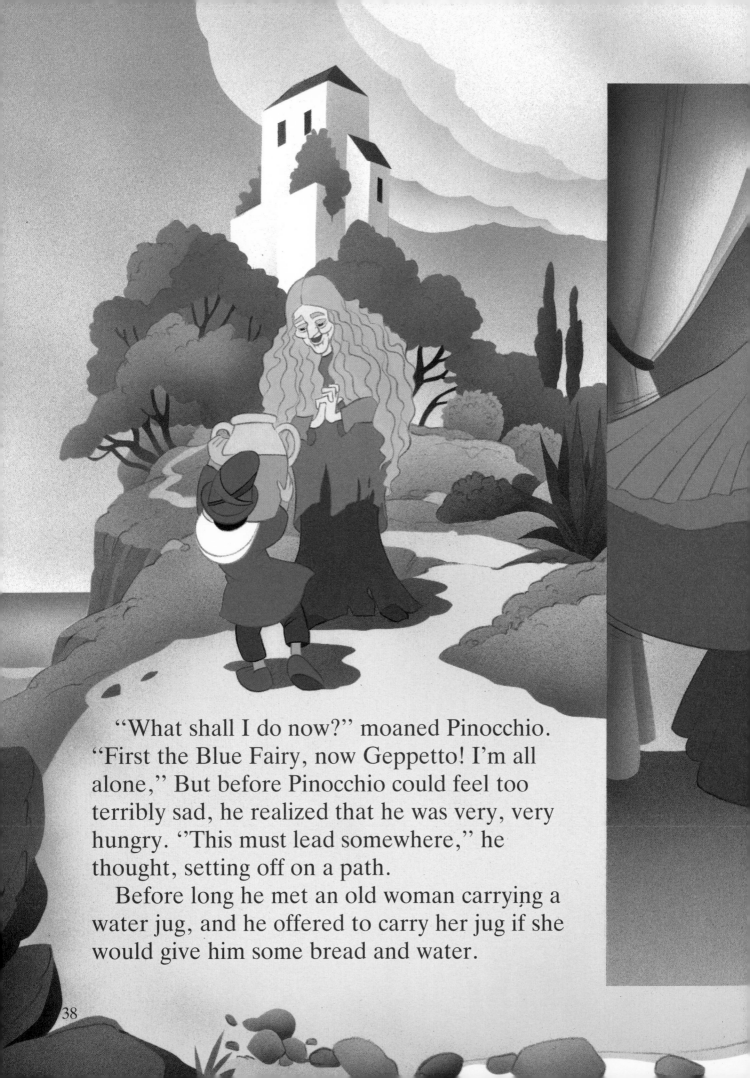

"What shall I do now?" moaned Pinocchio. "First the Blue Fairy, now Geppetto! I'm all alone," But before Pinocchio could feel too terribly sad, he realized that he was very, very hungry. "This must lead somewhere," he thought, setting off on a path.

Before long he met an old woman carrying a water jug, and he offered to carry her jug if she would give him some bread and water.

At the woman's house Pinocchio ate and drank his fill. When he looked up from his plate, he cried out in wonder. The old woman had changed into the Blue Fairy. "You're alive! You're here!" shouted Pinocchio joyfully.

After they hugged, the Blue Fairy told Pinocchio she would care for him like a mother. He promised to try very hard to be good, and go to school.

The next day Pinocchio went to school, and the day after, and the day after that. He studied his books; he listened to the Blue Fairy; and helped with the chores. But one day on the way to school, the boys told Pinocchio they were going to see a great shark in the ocean near the beach. Pinocchio thought of Geppetto, and decided to join the boys.

But when they reached the sea, no shark could be seen. When the boys began to laugh, Pinocchio realized they had tricked him. Then they teased Pinocchio, and the boys began to fight.

Then a boy hit on the head by a book fell to the ground. The other boys ran away. Pinocchio stayed to help the hurt boy. But when a policeman came and accused Pinocchio, he ran away in fear.

It was dark when the frightened puppet made his way all the way back to the village, and knocked on the Blue Fairy's door. A snail poked its head out the window.

"I'mm Pinocchio! Let me in!" cried the puppet.

It took the snail, being as slow as all snails are, until morning to open the door. While he waited, Pinocchio had lots of time to think of how his naughty behavior brought nothing but trouble.

Pinocchio decided the change. In the weeks that followed
he behaved well, and went to school every day. One day the
Blue Fairy announced, "Pinocchio, you are ready at last.
Tomorrow your great wish will come true. You'll turn into a
real boy! Let's have a party to celebrate. You may go invite
your friends, but come back before dark."

Pinocchio set off to invite his friends. But when he invited his mischievous friend, Lampwick, the boy replied, "Well, good luck to you, Pinocchio. I can't come though, because I'm running away for Funland. The wagon is coming to pick me up tonight, with all the other boys. Every day is a holiday in Funland, filled with games, rides and candy!"

Although Pinocchio tried to resist, when the wagon appeared, loaded with happy boys and pulled by donkeys, Lampwick and the coachman convinced the wayward puppet to join them.

All the way to Funland, Pinocchio thought of the Blue Fairy, and how he had behaved so well that she was going to make him a real boy. "I'll go home tomorrow," he thought. But as soon as he and Lampwick were in Funland, they were carried away by the endless games and sweets. Suddenly one day the boys were horrified to see that they had grown donkey ears.

Before long the miserable boys had changed completely into donkeys, for that was the fate of all boys in Funland. The cruel coachman then sold Pinocchio to a circus, where the ringmaster taught the donkey tricks. On his first night performing, Pinocchio sprained both his front legs so badly that he couldn't walk.

"I've paid good money for you," growled the ringmaster. "And now you're no good to me at all!" The man tied a heavy rock to Pinocchio's neck and pushed him over a cliff into the sea.

But the seawater magically changed the donkey into a puppet again and the rock slipped from his neck. Pinocchio swam away from the shore.

"What a close call!" thought Pinocchio. But his troubles were not over, for suddenly an enormous shark appeared. "Help!" cried Pinocchio. As he flailed in the water, the monstrous shark opened its cavernous mouth.

Pinocchio swam flat out, but the shark was faster. It caught up with Pinocchio and drew in its breath, sucking Pinocchio into a whirlpool of water that plunged down into the shark's belly.

It was dark and wet in the shark's belly.
"Help!" cried Pinocchio. "Oh, poor me!"
"Who is that?" asked a voice.
Pinocchio's despair turned suddenly to joy, for
there, floating in his little boat, was Geppetto.

After their tearful reunion, Pinocchio said, "Papa, we must escape from this awful place."

"But how?" asked Geppetto. "I don't know how to swim."

"I can help, if you show me the way," came a voice. Beside them surfaced a tunafish that had been swallowed in the same gulp with Pinocchio. The two climbed on the fish's back and made their way through the shark's throat and out his mouth, which was open as he slept.

Geppetto and Pinocchio rode comfortably on the tuna's back until they reached land. Then they thanked the helpful fish, and bade him good-bye.

Pinocchio helped his weak and trembling papa home, carrying him much of the way. Once there, he tucked Geppetto in bed and fed him hot soup. "I will take care of you now," said Pinocchio. "I will go to school, and I'll work to make money for us to live on."

"Pinocchio, you are so changed!" exclaimed Geppetto.

Pinocchio worked hard from that day on, doing his studies and his chores, and weaving baskets to make money for food. Geppetto slowly began to get better, and they shared many happy moments together. Then one day, the Blue Fairy appeared. "Brave, kind Pinocchio!" she said. "With your tender care and hard work, you have proved that your heart is good."

"You deserve to become a real boy now," said the Fairy
with a smile.

With a cry of delight, Pinocchio found that he was no
longer a wooden puppet, but a real live boy. He ran to
embrace Geppetto.

"My son," said Geppetto. "It is a happy day indeed!"